# *What Death Do We Part?*

By: E. Jene Harris

# *<u>Dedication</u>*

I would like to dedicate this book to all the dreamers out there. Never give up on your dream, no matter how long it takes you to get it done. Just make a decision and do it and do it right then.

## Table of Contents

## *Intro…*

The sight of him gave me fever. I mean sweat beading up on my forehead, cross my legs to stop my clit from throbbing, would jump his bones in the back of this church fever. His smooth skin made me crave chocolate and his smile was infectious. The thoughts running through my head in that moment as I sat facing my husband's congregation could only be described as sinful.

Don't get me wrong, despite my husband's spotless reputation, he was far from perfect. Still, was I really willing to go as far as committing adultery? That little voice in my head fought with me to decide.

On one hand, I could just tell that man had at least 8 inches to console me on my failing marriage. I knew this because of the many times I had stared at his crouch as he walked pass me, and the grey sweats he wore every Saturday to work out with a group at the church gym. His shoulders looked like I could sit all my troubles plus a few body parts of my choice on them.

On the other hand, as my doting husband never failed to remind me in his jealous fits, "God will punish the unfaithful". His suspicions only led me to believe that he himself had some outside dealings but since I had yet to discover the full truth of that revelation, I could only speculate.

*That being said, an eye for an eye, right? Or what he doesn't know, won't hurt me. Whichever would keep my conscious clear as I climbed this tree of a man and rode him like the very first cowgirl to do it. No, that wouldn't be right. I'm a married woman and a woman of God at that. No, I can get everything I need from my husband.* I reasoned with myself as church came to an end.

I found myself waiting in the parking lot. Not for my husband, because he had other church business to attend to and had said he'd be home in a couple of hours. Not even for my children, they had left with my husband's relatives for the night. No, I was waiting for him. We had managed to make plans after my husband let me know not to expect him to leave with me. I spotted him making his way towards me and was immediately conflicted. I couldn't understand why because he wasn't the first man I had gone out with during my miserable ass marriage. I couldn't put my finger on it, but something was different about this time.

As this man walked towards me, my clit grew a pulse and I knew it was over for me.

"You ready to go?" His voice vibrated through me and tickled my pussy with anticipation.

I smiled. "Yes, I'm ready."

The end usually says a lot about the beginning. This was the beginning of the end; but only by going back to the beginning can you understand why the end is what it is.

# **<u>Chapter One</u>**

## *In the Beginning*

In wedding vows, it says "until death do us part". Most people think that it's referring to a physical death; like when you're buried in the ground. In marriage, rather… being in the wrong marriage, there are so many more deaths that part you. You lose your mind, your identity, your passion, your drive, your ambition. The dreams and goals that you once had. Sometimes, you lose yourself. Sometimes you lose your self-worth because you're trying to keep it together. Women especially, we lose who we are in becoming a wife and/or a mother. We are no longer a woman and we forget our needs. At least, that's how the story usually goes; but this is a different story. Just as much drama as a reality show because this is unscripted; and one packed with more juice than the box in your child's lunchbox because I had that just that much going on. Let me fill you all in.

Today, I'll be hosting a few rounds of my show's version of the newly-wed, so it's only right that I rehash the details of my sorted past. That way it will be fresh on my mind as I get these questions together for the couples playing. Maybe I should just start at the beginning, so you can understand my point of view when it comes out at the panel. Believe me, I have a lot to say.

The beginning of a relationship is a unique thing. It can feel like everything you've ever wanted and having planning your future around what you think is perfection. Don't get me wrong, I'm not saying that relationships are all bullshit in the beginning. I'm just saying if you're not careful, it can have you so fooled. You'll be thinking you're getting yourself into one thing, when really... it's something else completely. This is the case too often.

I met my ex-husband in college. We met at the end of our junior year, going into our senior year. He was kind of goofy to me, but he was sweet. He always sent nice gestures early in the morning and I thought that was cute. So, it went on for several months before I agreed to go on a date with him.

So, we finally went on a date after about six or seven months of us chatting back and forth, seeing each other at school and being in a class or two together. We went into our senior year and started "kind of" dating. We would go out more, but weren't exactly serious yet. By that time, I had bought my first house at age 20 and was getting ready to graduate with my second degree at 21. I also already had my first child. My daughter was about four or five. Our relationship got stronger because we had so many accomplishments in common. We both had good jobs, our cars were paid off. We each had just purchased new homes and were a month away from graduation. We had plans to start businesses of our own and set other goals to accomplish together. Sounds Ideal, right? That's the thing about beginnings...they sometimes have very little in common with endings.

As you would expect, with all that going right... we decided to be a couple and build together. I wanted a household where there was mom, dad and children; or more specifically…mom, step-dad, and my daughter. Then if we got married, I would have another kid and we would be one happy family. It was what the goal was for both of us.

Before I go any further, let me lay out the dynamics of his background. Everybody in his family was all Holy and in God. The whole family. If you didn't have a title, you needed to get one. For me, this eventually became an issue because I knew who and what I was. No one could make me stop being me. I wasn't about to convert nor conform.

So, we got into the relationship and decided not to have sex before getting married because he was a minister. He proposed to me that next November during a big Thanksgiving dinner party at my cousin Lisa's house. He had it all planned out and everyone was in on it. He asked my daughter if he could marry me by first giving her a ring. Then, he got down on one knee and made a memory.

All eyes were on me and giving me my ring. Everybody was a ball of tears. He took my hand and looked into my eyes. "Every day with you, I learn something new about myself. You bring out the best in me. So, naturally…I want to keep you around for the rest of my life. Will, you do me the honor of having you as my wife?"

I was a ball of emotion and "yes" couldn't pour from my lips enough times. We were officially engaged and everything seemed to be going as we had planned it out in our minds.

We got married four months later in March. It was a beautiful outdoor wedding with about 300 guests. We had so much fun and all of our family came together to celebrate our love. I just knew this would last a lifetime. That was the beginning, I had my goals, I had my little girl and now I had my guy. The only question left to ask was, what now. Better yet, what's the move

## Chapter Two

*What's the Move?*

He moved into my house before we actually got married. We chose my home because it had more bedrooms. Therefore, he had a room, my daughter had a room, I had a room, and we had a spare room. The house was on a half-acre of land in a nice neighborhood out in the old country Mississippi. We were trying to do it God's way, so even when he moved in before the wedding, there was no sex.

After we got engaged, we went to marriage counseling, of course with somebody in his church. I had a mega-church that I was deeply involved in as well; but he wouldn't agree to getting counseling at that church. I wasn't more adamant about it because I didn't want to come off as trying to start confusion before we got going in the marriage.

The first year was nice, but it wasn't long before I found out that sex was not his strong point. Our first time together was all fumbles and frustration. He laid on top of me struggling to get with the rhythm. I was struggling as well, but my battle was keeping my facial expression from giving away my thoughts.

"Damn baby, I knew this kitty was going to be good. I knew it." He grunted as his stiff strokes somehow gave him confidence. "Did you know it would be this good too?"

"Umhm." It was all I manage to say. I just knew if I opened my mouth, the words that came out would hurt his feelings. I pulled him closer to me and hoped that it was just first-time nervousness.

He was a nice size, but he had no idea of how to work it. If he would have put in any work at all, he would have been a beast. Instead he made me feel as if he was not attracted to me and that I didn't turn him on. Needless to say, I knew right away that I would need to invest in Duracell or look up annulments. Between me and you, I check my stock every day.

By that next December, we had our son; he had gotten a job promotion and I found a job on base as a Navy Contractor. So, despite the small issues we had in our marital bed...we were moving forward and the next move was moving to another state. There, in Jacksonville, FL, is where things took a turn for the worse. We had to basically start over. We had no family over there. We had to just rely on each other; but we were super excited to be moving to a new city and state that we had loved to visit and vacation to as well as the financial upgrade we were about to take part in. So, as a newly-wed couple with two kids, we were super happy about the move.

We worked all the time. *I get it, we both had just gotten new and really well-paying jobs, so we both had to be in "beast mode"; but did we have to forget about our marriage? In my mind, we were way to early into the marriage to become comfortable neglecting one another.* So, I would remind him. "Let's do a date night or take a trip." His response would always be, "I need to focus." I understood that, but he had a whole family that had moved over with him, we needed his time as well. Especially, his wife. I was feeling like we had completely skipped the honeymoon phase. He was neglecting all of my needs, all of them. *Some of which I could over look, but getting fucked should not have been an issue in a new marriage.* I knew he was a minister but he should have known how to find balance. You have to take care of your spouse, just like you take care of the church and your job. *Don't neglect me.* There was plenty of dick being offered to me, just not by my husband. That's what planted the seeds that would eventually uproot everything we had planned.

So, we began to argue more consistently than we made love. It was really out of frustration for me. He wasn't trying to help me release all this stress that I had all built up inside of me. Any other man would have been more than ready to cause this waterworks to flow all over them. We were both tired. I didn't work as many hours as he did, but I made decent money. I worked and took care of the kids and had to go to church to support that side of his life, but my physical needs were nowhere on his damn agenda.

So, there we were, in a new state, with only each other and yet we still managed to turn against one another. The move was definitely not "the move" I had expected it to be. Looking back now, it was really inevitable that something would happen. Especially, with the way I was feeling.

Every married couple will tell you that temptation always rears its ugly head the moment you let doubt in. At that moment, I was seriously doubting my marriage and sincerely frustrated. Enter, temptation.

# <u>**Chapter Three**</u>

*Temptation and Revelation*

All that marriage counseling we took before getting married and not one of those sessions was about fighting temptation. It made me wonder if I was the only church wife that wasn't getting pleased physically. I mean, yes, the bills were being taken care of. Yes, there was also a lot of money being spent. Financially, we were more than stable, but no I wasn't happy. The money may have been enough for a different kind of woman. Whatever kind that is, I'm for sure not that kind. I worked, took care of the kids, the house, him. I cooked, cleaned, and did my minister's wife duties (going to all the meetings, the teas, the fundraisers, the conferences, the meetings about meetings, choir rehearsals, praise and worship practices). Anything that they could make up to keep you at church. I deserved comfort, spoiling…shit I at least deserved orgasms.

I'm an attractive woman if I do say so myself, so of course it wasn't long before the men of the church started to take notice. My husband insisted on being in attendance for every event or meeting the church held. So, of course we were members of the church's work-out group.

Then this one day, I was summoned to the gym by a friend who was also a drummer at the church. My husband had to work; but he and his family still expected me to be there because it was a church event. I was looking good in my yoga pants and crisp white wife-beata…not to brag but you can't hide all these curves.

All of the men snuck glances when the opportunity arose, but I noticed one of them paying a little more attention. He flashed me a smile and I smiled back. I guess he took that as his que to come over and start a conversation; because the next thing I knew he was headed in my direction.

The first thing about him that caught my attention was the bulge in his sweats. "Good God…please give me the strength." I mumbled to myself as he approached.

"Hi, I'm Jonathan. May I have the pleasure of knowing your name?" His smooth voice made me instantly wet.

"I'm Pam. Nice to meet you." I looked right into his eyes like no one around us knew my husband.

"Believe me, the pleasure is all mine." He openly let his eyes roam down my body then back up. "And to think I was against coming to this church group when my homeboy invited me."

I raised an eyebrow. "Have a change of heart?"

"Definitely. Listen, I can't walk away without shooting my shot. Can I take you out some time?" I could see the hope in his eyes.

I looked around, expecting some of the nosey female members of the church to be all eyes and ears in my direction. To my surprise, they were all too busy struggling through their workouts. I hate to admit it but I was really standing there eying this fine ass man weighing my options. *Could I really get away with seeing him behind my husband's back? Was I really willing to risk it all?* He bit down on his full bottom lip and there was no more debating it. "Sure, but only if you agree never to come to this group again." I lick my lips. "A lady likes to be discrete."

He leaned in and half-whispered. "Shit, I wasn't planning on coming back anyway. Just slide me your number baby…and I'll be on my way right now."

I whispered my number to him and walked away. I didn't have to look back to know his eyes were on my ass.

There were other frustrations on top of my dissatisfaction. Outside of work, we were involved in his church full-time. I knew I could use one of the church events he had to work during to make some of what I was planning to call me time. My husband wouldn't notice, he rarely paid attention to me. He was now moving into assistant pastoring the pastor- a woman by the way… so it was like he was working two full-time jobs instead of one. I could definitely get away with it. So much for fighting temptation; but this was the least of my problems in my marriage.

I was the type of wife and woman that could discern spirits. I could walk into a room and I knew who was for me (or us) and who wasn't. I knew, I felt that something underlying had a hold on us, something was missing. Something was not right. It felt like a heavy spirit was on us. We both knew and felt it… but we ignored it. We acted as if everything was great. Like we were happy. Like we were living the good life but at night, we went to bed with our backs toward each other. Then there were the stares; and walking pass each other was some bullshit to say the least. Still, we had to keep up appearances for the church and family members.


     Being introduced to people that worked under him at the church, there was one woman named Barbara who I still love to this day. Ten or eleven years later, we are still good friends. She now tells me stuff that I felt was going on back then but couldn't get solid evidence for. She felt she couldn't say while it was occurring because she didn't want to be the cause of drama in our marriage. Barbara has really looked out for me and been a really good person toward me since I met her. Over the years, I've became closer with her whole family.


     There was another woman I was introduced to that we will call "T", who had a thing for my husband. Now, my husband wasn't ugly…he was just a little out of shape. Despite that, he could still be described as tall, dark and handsome. Plus, he made a lot of money. You know when a man makes a lot of money and has a little authority, ladies act like groupies. Besides, the money, he had always been a real gentleman and a nice guy…I can't take that from him. We were just on different levels when were together. In the end, he became emotional and petty but that doesn't take away from the fact that he was still a good guy. At some points, he just chose to take the bad guy route in some situations…but that's men in general right? Back to "T". When I met her, I didn't even shake her hand. That's so not my character, I usually love most people. Her, I just couldn't do.

That night at dinner, I told him. "That girl is going to be an issue for us, but if I catch her or you out of line, just know y'all coming up missing."

As my husband introduced us, it seemed as if my name sparked something in her mind. I saw her little ears perk up like a hound dog on a scent trail. While she acted glad to meet me, I knew there was something else behind it. I didn't have to wait long to find out either. I went to the bathroom to pee and as I was in the stall, I heard someone walk in on a phone call.

"Yeah, her name is Pam. I don't know if that's her or not…I'll see if I can sneak and get a picture. Yeah…shit he ain't cute but he's paid. I'll play ball for a while if need be. You just make sure she's the one. I don't want his fat ass touching me for nothing. Let me go, I gotta see if she left so I can get this picture. I'll call you when I get home."

I watched through the crack in the stall door as "T" checked herself out in the mirror, pushed her titties up and blew herself a kiss. Then walked out humming a familiar tune.

Hearing my name had me feeling like I was caught in the matrix. *Who the hell had she been on the phone with? Why did she need a picture and more importantly, why the fuck was she talking about letting my husband touch on her?* It was all too much. I flushed the toilet, fixed my clothes and left the stall. I washed my hands as I checked myself out in the mirror. My titties were sitting up right, so I didn't need to push them up. "Hm." I laughed to myself. "If she wants a picture, it's gonna be a good one."

15

While hearing that conversation was a revelation in itself, I was sure that there would be more to come. Some marriages start out about kisses and compromise…mine was mostly temptations and revelations. One minute I would think we were making progress; the next, we were right back where we started.

# **Chapter Four**

## *Back Where We Started*

"Back to where we started." It's a phrase riddled with disappointment. Finding yourself back at a point you already worked to get pass or get over is one of the most frustrating things to deal with. Especially while trying to grow a healthy marriage.

For the most part, things were good. We were able to do a lot for our kids and travel because we made over six figures together. We had a nice home and enjoyed a quality of life some people never get to experience. Still, there were some underlying things that were keeping us from growing. We started out having disagreements about where church should fall on our agenda and priority lists…a year later we were right back having the same discussions. We had just taken the scenic route, through hell and high-water first.

One of the things that was a weight on our marriage was that the church overrode everything. We were in church five days a week. I even prayed that he would wake up one day and not want to be a minister. Even back in Mississippi we had gone to all these celebrity television bishop conferences and everybody was talking about God being good and putting you in the right place at the right time for the right blessing or breakthrough. How God will, God shall… God, God, God; but nobody talked about how to keep your marriage intact. They talked about the bed being undefiled, but really the bed is defiled. If you can't do any and everything to your spouse then the bed is defiled. After a while, saying "I love you" becomes just another one of your routines, your actions have to speak louder. *It was a sentiment that my dear husband just couldn't seem to grasp; but hey…who had time for relationship issues when there was so much to do at the church right?*

The leading pastor at this church was getting older but she was still well dressed, always in heels and pantyhose. I get that, I liked to dress as well. I would wear my skirt suits or dresses and heels but I didn't wear stockings or hats. My husband was always making refence to how I dressed. That I needed to wear more longer dresses, and lower heels, and put on a hat, and less form fitting outfits; and the church folks was in full agreement with him in their daily talks and eye rolls of my attire. Understand, I was not dressing like a whore but I was not dressing like they wanted me too. I would tell them how about work on what you look like and let's get soul saved instead of focusing on what I wear you, hypocrites ......ugh as I stormed out if the church meeting that was about me than the fake agenda they say they had.

After that that night, I look at them all with hate in my heart. I became more standoffish and I didn't talk to anyone else's after that. So now I have to be around these hell-bound church folks and I'm supposed to have a smile on my face and speak well of them. I hate it here.

He got so deep into the church that he wanted me to become a minister. The church had started all of the male ministers' wives in training, going to Bible school or theology and getting licenses to be ministers. I did it, but it wasn't for me. All the unrealistic expectations they put on you, I don't think God asks for all that. That just wasn't who

I am. I couldn't save people expecting me to be someone other than myself. Of course, this added to our growing pile of issues. I could not be this fake woman that they wanted me to portray. I could only be me and that's a real, transparent woman that has issues that I have learned from. One that's willing to offer help, wisdom and encouragement to the best my knowledge will allow.

People came to me more than they went to him because they could connect with me. They felt that they could trust me; that they could say what they wanted and needed to say and I would not judge them; but instead give them encouragement and wise counsel on whatever their situation was. All while still holding them accountable and responsible for whatever they were doing or not doing in their situation. I didn't condemn them to hell like he and the elders of that church did.

Church was just the tip of the iceberg on our issues though. We didn't communicate well, mostly because he tried to hide things from me. He spent more money than he had to while I was trying to grow our savings. I dealt with the kids mostly on my own because he was always at work or church and I wasn't getting any sex. I would get pissed off; no...I would get mad. Then I got to a point where I just said "fuck it, I'm tired". *If we weren't going to work things out, then "we" weren't going to work out.* Church was just another "death" that was causing us to part.

We were in Jacksonville for about three and a half years. We made great money and in other people's eyes...we were the ideal couple to be; but at home, it was cold. I was in passionless, fireless, sexless marriage, and I mean wasn't shit happening. We hadn't had sex in about six months and I was about to die. I was about to absolutely die behind the drought.

At this same time, I was going through our statements. *You know some shit is wrong when you have to talk out loud to your damn self.* So, I asked myself, "What in the hell was he spending $100 a day on lunch for?" He said he was treating some of the church members. When I first discovered this, my first thought was "you better not be spending our damn money on that bitch "T". He said he wasn't but I don't know what kind of fool he took me for, nobody spends $100 a day on lunch just for themselves.

It wasn't that we were financially strapped. We weren't living paycheck to paycheck, but that was $500 a week on just lunch. We still had to do breakfast and dinner together as a family. We were spending $1,500 a month on fucking food. *What, were we feeding a small country? What the hell was going on?* I was pissed the entire fuck off, so I decided to start monitoring our spending. I moved money over, calculating bills and breaking all of our spending down. We were not about to be spending $1,500 a month on some damn food.

We were young and making really good money and I had the bills under control; but I couldn't control his spending because he also had checks coming in that I would never see. So, I didn't have full control of his money. Plus, "T" was helping him spend a lot of our money before he even brought it home, my muthafuckin money.

I had to start popping up on him. See, I worked on base. So, he couldn't just pop up on me. Coming on base meant extensive searching for him and his car. If you didn't have a decal, you could guarantee yourself at least a two hour wait before you could even get through the gates. Then, I would have to come meet him at the gates and escort him in…in the company vehicle. Basically, he knew about my whereabouts but he couldn't get there. He, on the other hand, worked at a church. I could just pull up on him at any time. Part of me was saying, "No, Pam. Just pray about it." The rest of me was saying, "Hell to the damn no! Get yo ass over to that church and shut that shit down!" So, I started pulling up and just walking in like "what the fuck going on in here". It never failed, whenever I showed up, "T" was always in his office when I got there. He would have some excuse, "Oh, we had a meeting. Oh, we just got finished with this or that". The question was, why was she still in there when everybody else was at their got damned desk? Well, that was the first question. Really, I had so many. *Why the hell was she always in his office? What the fuck she got going on?* From day one, I knew she was going to be a problem. Any time I say something with no reason to say it, it's always comes true. It has not failed me yet; and again, I say…IT ALWAYS COMES TRUE.


I started pulling up at different times, every other day. I went to work on the base so as soon as I dropped the kids off every morning. I got to work early; but the people that made all the decisions didn't come in until damn near lunch time. By that time, I was finished with all my work. So, I bombarded them at their desks with all my stuff as soon as they got there. After that, I could leave at any time.


Usually, when I left for lunch…I didn't have to come back. The Navy wasn't that strict when it came to that. As long as you got your job done, your work was done right and they didn't have to come looking for you to do your job…they were cool with whenever you came or went. See, I was an early bird. I got in there at about seven am. So, from seven to twelve, I was hitting it hard. I would leave at twelve and stay gone until about three, if I came back at all. Even then, I was gone by four. I didn't have a set time to work, as long as my job was done. The people that stayed late would have their stuff on my desk by morning and I would get it all done by twelve. I had a system; I was in and out. So, he couldn't monitor when I would show up. He had a director that he had to answer to though, so he didn't have the flexibility that I had. That being said, popping up became second nature for me.

I would pull up on his ass and be like, "what the fuck's going on around here?" So, when they realized I was going to be pulling up at any time, "T" started staying away. That was when I turned to Barbara. I would take her to lunch and get the tea.

"Barbara, why the fuck is she always in his office?"

She said she would try to stay in the office with them and make sure that "T" got reminded that he had a wife.

I was like, "Girl, you better let that heffa know because these are problems."

Barbara would suggest we sought a little counseling and let me know that "T" was pressing him, not the other way around. Still, this was a grown ass man who could tell her to sit the fuck down as needed. Of course, I asked if "T" and my husband had ever gone to lunch together. Barbara said that they would go, but always with other people. I needed to know. *Were they going together?* Like, *was she getting in the car that I helped pay for? Where were they gong? And again, who the fuck had she been talking to on the phone that day?* Barbara let me know that they were going out to lunch together often.

On one of these pop ups, I was able to get the answer to one of my questions. The day I first met "T", I made sure she was able to "sneak" a great picture of me when she thought I wasn't looking. I needed to know who her and the mystery caller thought I was. It took months for me to get an answer, but the bathroom stall came through again. This time, she had the caller on speaker as she washed her hands. "I keep telling you not to worry, girl. I'll get him to give me some money and send you a couple dollars. He spends like there's no tomorrow, and his bitch has no clue. The least she can do is let her husband help you with a bill or two after stealing the love of your life."

"Bitch, every time I think about it, I want to hit somebody. His ass dropped me like a bad habit when she sashayed her fat ass under his big country nose. She left his ass when the next best opportunity rose, but he ain't never look my way again. She may not have even wanted him for real to begin with; but his fine ass got a good job now and I can't help but to wonder what my life might be like had we gone through with our plans to get married before college."

"Girl, that stuff never works out anyway. Who knows, y'all might have been divorced by now; but I'm happy to help my big sis get a little revenge on a bitch. Especially, when I get paid in the process. Let me go, girl. I gotta let his ass feel me up before the staff meeting. I'm starting to feel a little bad for the fat ass. All it takes a quick whiff of pussy and he's hemorrhaging money."

"Shit! Well, you be the nurse and sop all that change up. Call me later, sis."

"You know I will."

Again, I watched her blow herself a kiss in the mirror before walking out. I sat there for a minute trying to remember what guy they might be talking about. The only one that came to mind was Jarrod England, the star quarterback. We got all hot and nasty junior year, but when he hurt his knee and they benched him, I moved on. I mean, I'm not shallow by any means, but those high school things never work anyway. Somebody should have told ole' girl on the phone that. After all these years, she was still holding a grudge about a boy back in high school? *Silly rabbit.* I flushed, fixed my clothes, washed my hands and left the bathroom. Now that I had confirmed "T" and my husband had a "thing", I no longer needed to pop up. Still, I made one more surprise trip.

This time, I only stopped by my husband's office just to let her know I was there. I just knew she was going to rush to the bathroom to call her sister. When she did, I was already in there waiting. No stall this time though. This time I hid behind the door so she wouldn't see it coming.

When she went to blow herself that first kiss in the mirror I reached over and bashed her head right into her own reflection, cracking the mirror in the process. I wanted to let the bitch know it was me but I couldn't risk her pressing charges. Instead I slipped out and left feeling satisfied.

Honestly, I wasn't tripping at that point. The drought was about to be over for me. I pulled out my phone and dialed the number to that fine ass muthafucka I had met at the church work out group and sent him a text. *Hey, what's good for the gander has to be good for the goose too...right?*

**Hey there handsome. I guess it's time to play a little game.**

I rushed home to shower and change into something more first date appropriate and made my way to the designated meeting spot... his place. To be fair, even though I was wrong for entertaining him all together...I wasn't about to lead him into believing we were starting a relationship. I was only interested in one thing for the moment.

"Hey." He flashed his winning smile when he opened the door.

"Hey yourself." I smiled back then slipped by him and walked inside, making sure to rub against him as I did.

"Damn." He said out loud.

"I don't have a lot of time; my kids will be getting out of school in another hour and a half." I looked around at his tastefully decorated apartment, then took a seat on his couch.

"Ummm..okay. I'm new at this sort of thing. Where do you want to start?" His question was amusingly cute.

I opened my legs, revealing that I hadn't bother wearing any panties. "Start on your knees."


You may as well say that me and the husband were back to just dating. He had his extracurricular activities and now I had mine. No, we had gone all the way back to were we started...the begin...only seeing each other when we had time. That us when we weren't thot-scotching...

# <u>Chapter Five</u>

*Thot-scotching and State Hopping*

*Thot-scotching- going back and forth in sexual relationships.* While my husband and I had no intentions of getting a divorce, our extra-curricular activities were at an all-time high. He had his high school sweetheart and of course "T" and I was surrounded by handsome men to choose from every day at work and I did take my choice.

There was also this sexy ass dude that worked on base. I mean, I worked on a Naval base with mostly men. So, there was always something nice to look at in any direction I looked; but there was a sexy little something that was looking at me and yeah...I went to lunch with him a whole lot. I had been telling him what was going on and he was becoming a listening ear when I needed to vent. Yes, I did have a crush on him and I knew he liked me too but there was nothing going on between us. This was strictly business. We had even partnered in a lot of different outside ventures. Outside of the Navy, he did a lot of work in the entertainment business. So, through him, I was able to put money into certain ventures to make some money come back and increase for the family. He wrote plays and I was an actress in them, or I would sing background I sine of his tracks sometimes. He was a good friend.

There was also this other guy who called me his "work-wife"; he was a really cool dude. Very sweet and gentleman-like. He always had my back but he was not attracted to me. He was just really a good dude. After pulling up on my husband for about three weeks, I understood that this was what he was going to be doing, so I said let me do it too. Now, I didn't have to do it, but it was on my mind to. Especially, because I hadn't gotten any from him for about a year. I felt like this was some bullshit. So, these guys were paying for everything, talking to me, writing poems for me and about me. Inviting me to different places to see them perform pieces that they had written for me. I was relishing all the attention.

The shit was sexy, it got me wet. *I mean what do you do? Your husband is seeing another woman, he's not having sex with you. You got to get it somehow, right?* I knew for a fact that "T" was having sex with my husband because my security detail crew had recorded them in the act on several occasions in hotel rooms. They've even replayed recordings of him making her promises to leave me so they could become a power couple. She promised him she would make a better first lady than me. He couldn't have seen what I saw, because when I would bring her up...he would get mad. Whatever, it was cool. It wasn't like he was giving her good sex. *Or was he? Was he giving her the "d" he was supposed to be giving his wife?* The reason I got pregnant so fast was simply because I was fertile. That's why I had to get my tubes tied. We had sex on our honeymoon and nine months later, we had our son. We weren't even married a year before the baby came because I was just that fertile. So, what I was doing had nothing to do with jealousy and everything to do with fairness. *Afterall, I was a reflection of him.*

So, being on the Navy base with all these fine ass men, a few of them really liked me. I was totally taking advantage too because I was always going to lunch with somebody different. The girl who worked in the office next to me stopped me one day and said, "yo, you're being reckless." In my defense, I wasn't sleeping with any of the men I worked with. Still, she said I was being "reckless". But if I was being so reckless, why was I so happy?

# <u>Chapter Six</u>

*Why Are You Happy?*

About six months of this and my husband finally asked me, "Why are you so happy?" *What the fuck do you mean why am I so happy?* He knew that he wasn't doing anything to please me, yet I wasn't sad or depressed. That was because there were other guys that had my eyes open. Not that I was cheating physically with all of them, but yes, I was taking overnight trips. My homegirl was going with me but I was going along to entertain.

Let me pause for clarity, because I know you're wondering if he was out and I was out...who the hell had the kids? There were other people keeping my kids or sometimes I paid to fly my mom in, or sister...somebody. We made enough money that I could drop about five or six hundred dollars for a family member to come spend the weekend with my children. *I could afford it, so why not?* I wasn't paying for any of the trips that I was going on with these men and I wasn't sleeping with them either because me and my homegirl would always get the room together. I would be with her in the room but go out with them.

*Okay, okay.* A couple of times, yes, I did go to their rooms; and yes, they kissed and licked me up; BUT WE DID NOT HAVE SEX. They did what they did because they knew that I had no sexual relationship with my husband and we weren't even two or three years into the marriage. *That's crazy as fuck.*

There eventually came a time that we went to counseling with the pastor's brother and his wife. They came to the house with other couples and we had a marriage retreat right there at our house. We tried to work on the marriage and it worked out for about two months. Then, it was back to nothing. Sex wasn't good at all. When I say the sex wasn't good, I mean… no touching, no kissing. It was like we were having one long-ass one-night-stand. I never reached an orgasm, just emptiness. Emotionless, just sad. I tried to talk him about it. I even asked him what was I doing wrong. *What could I do better? What was it?* He said it was good to him. *Yeah, because you're cumming in like 32 seconds. I need more! I couldn't figure out how to express my displeasure without rubbing his ego the wrong way.* So, this was an issue that went unaddressed. Orally pleasing me still hadn't grown on him, so that couldn't replace what his dick wasn't doing. It was just ugly.

The counseling in itself turned out to be an experience we didn't see coming. The session included two other couples that came from another church. After a few exercises, we were all asked to share some of our issues with the groups.

"She can't seem to tell me the truth about anything." One of the husbands said right away.

"Maybe if you didn't bitch about every single thing, I would want to tell you shit." His wife jumped in right behind him.

My husband and I exchanged glances.

"Do any of the other couples have any suggestions about how to resolve this issue?" The group leader asked to our surprise.

"You have to make her comfortable telling you things. It sounds like she just doesn't like disappointing you." My husband said with a shrug.

"But you have to stop lying, girl. Don't you want him to trust you?" I added.

The group burst into discussion and the leader brought it full circle with a Bible verse of course. Then the leader asked the group again for any volunteers to share issues they might be going through.

"Outside of sex, she is cold emotionally. Like she only thinks I worth the orgasm." Another husband complained.

I had to fight a frown because I would have killed for that to be my issue.

"It's not like you're that emotionally welcoming." His wife responded. "Your mind is always on work. So, I'm happy to catch you horny."

"Shoot, she could not want to have sex with you at all. Y'all men have to learn to make time to take care of your wife's physical and emotional needs." I said, more to my husband than I believe even he recognized.

"Right, providing is a great quality, but we need to connect sometimes." His wife added.

After a few more discussions and Bible verses, the session ended and the leader came to us with a big smile on his face. "You two were great today."

For the first time in a long time, we actually smiled at each other and agreed that we wouldn't be able to get what we needed from a group where we had all the best advice with as fucked up as our marriage was. How did that work? We couldn't revive the dying areas of our marriage but we could help everybody else to work towards thriving relationships.

Then, he lost his job. He told me that he lost his job because "they wanted to put somebody else in that position"; but in reality, he lost his job because that "T" heifer went to the pastor and board members and told them about the romantic relationship that she was having with their precious assistant pastor and director of the church financial ministry. She single-handedly took us down, I wondered if that scar on her face had caused the change of heart. The church was in total shock for multiple reasons. For one, she had just had a terrible bicycle accident causing a gash on her cheek. Now she had to endure sexual harassment right there in the church. On top of all that, they had been so busy tearing me down; they had never expected him to be the problem. I bet their jaws dropped when they saw the pictures and videos she had snuck during their interactions, all the bank transfers from all the money he had given her. After that, all those same folks at the church that had been judging and looking down on me, were trying to be nice. *Man, get the fuck out my face!*

We ended up moving back to Mississippi to the house we still owned from when we first graduated college. When we left, we allowed our family, well his family, to move into our homes and pay the mortgages. Come back to my house to find out the muthafuckas had been missing payments on my shit. It wasn't but $685 a got damn month had my house going into foreclosure. A brand-new house. So, the first thing I had to do was fix all that shit, but since I had moved money around the way that I did, we were able to live off that money for a couple of years. He didn't know that though. I made him get a job. I got a job too, but I had to hide money from him because he had horrible spending habits.

Now that we were back in Mississippi, we got back into church mode and he got back into preaching. They wanted me to start speaking, all while we were supposed to be working on our relationship. We tried to work on it but the sex was never there. Communication was better, we would take little trips, but I wasn't happy and he acted as if he wasn't happy either. Most likely because we had already been through so much, and we could have come back from it because I was willing to work for it. I never wanted to get married and then divorced, I felt that we should grow together. Like let's really do this. Of course, he listened to his family, I didn't listen to mine because mine didn't know what was going on until after the fact. Not until after the fact of all this going on.

We were back in Mississippi, living in my house along with other people. Living with other people meant I had to see his brother on a daily basis and he was still trying to sleep with me; pushing me into empty rooms, saying "I know you want me because I know my brother ain't giving you the "D" like you need. He's always been a square like that." I would push him out of my way; but in the back of my head, I was like "OMG, we have to get out of here before I take him up on that offer!" The offer that came daily, sometimes twice daily. We had to get the hell out of that house.

So, after realizing that wasn't going to work, we moved his family out of his house and we moved into that house with our kids. I hated it. I hated the way they had done his house, so I did everything over and he didn't like it. I told him that I wanted to move back into my house, I wanted my house back. Plus, even though we had moved out of the house his brother was in, he was still just around the corner. He was always outside harassing me during my daily jogs… even if my kids came along. I had to get him away from that side of town. I had to come up with a plan, so I did. I bitched and complained about that for like seven months until he agreed to tell his mother and other family that they had to move out of my house. We moved back into my house and another set of his family members moved into his house because his mother and that set had found their own house. It was stupid, but I had to get rid of his brother.

All in all, we stayed in church all the time and there were some adjustments but we just never bounced back from Jacksonville. So, after about a year, we moved to Los Angeles, CA. We moved mostly because his family said God told us to move. I was all for it because I was ready to get the hell on.

We left that summer and my aunt had a house there she wasn't using. So, we used that as our "extended stay", until everybody found their own apartment. Eventually, everyone found an apartment somewhere close to each other and I got into T.V. Somewhere along the way I decided I wanted to be a T.V show host and it happened really fast. I was doing it, on a gospel station of course because I had to go with what the family would approve of, anything for a new beginning right?

# <u>Chapter Seven</u>

*New Beginnings?*

So, I met up with some awesome people. I was doing my thing. I was going out for sponsorships because I needed them, just like with anything that you do, that's how T.V works. Corporate sponsors, individual sponsors, private sponsors, small business sponsors. Whatever the case maybe, you need sponsorship. I was working this little restaurant job at a little "mom and pop" place that only had me there enough that I could make a little money. He had gotten another job with a church when we got to Los Angeles, so I didn't need to make much. This job worked for me because there were a lot of people that came in there who made some decent money and own businesses in the area.

So, I met a couple of people and I gave them my pitch and paperwork from the T.V station. A good amount of people was with it, they were taking packages. There was one guy names Mack. Now, let me say this, Mack was fine as hell; 6'3, chocolate brown and built like...damn. The nigga was just fine as fuck. Mack had a real estate business that he and his best friend had been partnering in for years. So, of course, I don't think they supported me because they needed the advertisement. They had been in business long enough to have that shit going on. They did it because Mack liked me.

Yes, Mack took me to a lot of expensive restaurants and a lot of other places. Yes, Mack started getting feelings for me and yes, I started getting feeling for him as well. I wasn't getting it a home, so it just developed, even though Mack was married and so was I. I told him that if we were going to build something, we both needed to get divorces…if that was really what we were going to do. I already know, nine out of ten times…ain't no man about to leave their wife and ain't no woman about to leave their husband. No matter how good the feeling got. I wasn't and he wasn't but that's the shit we would tell each other because that's the shit the you tell each other to add to the fantasy. *Right?* Just to see how crazy the other person really is to do some shit and the other person not follow through on their end.

At the same time, my husband's brother's wife needed a job. Yes, the same brother that was trying to give me the "d" back in Mississippi. I wasn't really cool with her because she was a bit messy. All of them were really, so I kind stayed to myself. If I had a friend in the city than I would hang with them but never really the family. I got my sister-in-law a job with me and we pretty much worked the same hours and we lived right down the street from the location.

So, she would see Mack come in; so, when she started, I was like, "Listen, this girl is my husband's brother's wife. So, don't be hugging me or kissing at me like you used to do before she started working here because she's going to try to say some shit." There was something going on but it wouldn't be exactly what she would think it is because we did have a business relationship. I had business dealings with his company which included his wife, his homeboy and his homeboy's wife. I told him that we would get time outside of my place of work, but at that time he was so into me that when he saw me, he just ran up to me and was grabbing me. I let him know again that he had to stop that.

She would never say anything to me, she would just look at me when he came in. I would be like, "ooh, that thing is so fine but whatever let me gone back to work." So, I didn't know she was going back and making up complete lies. She had no reason to be messy that I knew of, but little did I know she had a few hundred.

She would say I would leave with him. Now, she knew that after she started working with me... I never left with him. He wasn't the only man that came in there and showed interest or flirted with me, but I guess he was the focus for her.

On a call with my favorite cousins on my dad's side brought on some new revelations my dear sister-in-law, Clarissa. "Wait a minute what do you mean, the tea on me?" I pressed my cousin Cecelia after she let it slip that my aunt had gotten "the tea" on me from Clarissa.

"Cousin, all I can say is that nobody is who they seem to be anymore."

"Un un, spill it." I pressed.

"Mama and Auntie Carolyn was talking one day about how you keep throwing money all around, buying plane tickets for yo mama and trying to show off that your marriage is going all good. Carolyn said, you know none of the women in this family can keep a man more than two years, so yo day is coming, but you didn't hear that from me."

"Right." I made a face as if she could see me. "What else did Auntie Carolyn have to say about me?"

"Mama mentioned that Clarissa had better make good on that money she gave her to expose you and your fake happiness before she gets the itch to let that church family y'all married into know who she used to be before marrying in."

"Wait, wait. She gave Clarissa money to expose me? What the fuck?"

"Yeah, but if you're really happy like I believe you are…ain't nothing her or Auntie Carolyn can do to change that. Don't let that bother you. You know those old women always doing something to make somebody unhappy like they are." My cousin tried to console me.

"Right." I said, with a sinking feeling in my heart. The messiness of the women on my father's side of the family was exactly why I had yet to tell any of my family how unhappy I really was in this marriage. Even with that being said, I never would have expected them to go this far to see me miserable. It's a shame, blood be the first to kick you when you're down. "And you heard Clarissa talking about me for yourself?"

"Hell yeah, with my own two ears. The bitch told us all about how you and that man were creeping off to have sex in the bathroom at your job. That's how mama got the idea to pay her to spill all the tea to your in-laws."

I couldn't believe my fucking ears. Part of me wanted to go back and forth with my cousin, setting her straight on every lie Clarissa's jealous ass had told, but I didn't have time for that. "Okay, girl. Let me get back to these kids. I'll call you tomorrow." I loved my cousin; she was one of the few on that side that I actually associated with closely. Still, this made me wonder what she might be saying behind my back if two of my "favorite" aunts could be doing me this dirty.

Clarissa had her reasons not to like me. She had mentioned to my cousin that she had a feeling her husband was into me. She said he would always ask her to ask me and only make a move if I said it was smart. Jealousy was just one of them. She was bigger than I was, I've always been thick but my shape is more curvy than big. My stomach is not flat but it's smaller than my butt. My breasts usually sit up and I usually have my hair really pretty. Most people say I have a really pretty smile. I love heels so I usually had a pair on. The heels give me a walk that some call the "nasty walk", my booty jiggles but that is all just a part of who I am. I wasn't putting on for any man in particular. Those are things I just can't change, that's just who I am. I was a dancer in high school, I was on a dance team in high school as well as college. So, I just had that walk because that's is what I'm used to. I walked on my tiptoes in dance and I wore heels. It is what it is. Bottom line, she was slightly jealous of me and how I looked versus how she looked; in addition to how all the people, men, women, white, black, whatever would seem to be attracted to me or want to talk to me. She would go to her husband (yes, the same husband that was always coming for me, trying to get these goodies) and our mother -in-law, telling them that I was not only sleeping with Mack but going with this guy and flirting with the next. She had a whole list of things that she claimed to have seen me doing. None of which was true. I wasn't sleeping with Mack. I was going out on dates with Mack, if that's what you want to call it. He would pay for everything. He sponsored my entire T.V show, I didn't want for anything. That is true. Yes, I've met him at his office before and he tried to have sex with me, but I would say no. Now, don't get me wrong. I was crazy about Mack because he was giving things (other than sex) that my husband wasn't able to give me. Little did Clarissa and my aunts know; I wore this thing right and made it look easy but my marriage was far from anything to be jealous of. I was at the beginning of the end of life as I knew it.

# **<u>Chapter Eight</u>**

## *The Beginning of the End*

Even while my marriage was deteriorating, church life was constant if nothing else. My fake smile was taking on a life of its own, it would appear with no effort on my part. I was at yet another church function, wishing I was anywhere else but pretending to be enthusiastic.

This time, it was a new members indoctrination. My husband was sitting on the alter beside the pastor so I had the pleasure getting a full look at the men joining the church first hand. There were a couple of good specimens, not that I had partaken in the congregation. I just enjoyed the views. I scanned the row of new members and one of them called for a second look...maybe even a third.

"Come church, give our new members a warm welcome." The pastor said as the new members made their way back to their seats among the rest of us.

The sight of him gave me fever. I mean sweat beading up on my forehead, cross my legs to stop my clit from throbbing, would jump his bones in the back of this church fever. His smooth skin made me crave chocolate and his smile was infectious. The thoughts running through my head in that moment as I sat facing my husband's congregation could only be described as sinful.

Don't get me wrong, despite my husband's spotless reputation, he was far from perfect. Still, was I really willing to go as far as committing adultery? That little voice in my head fought with me to decide.

On one hand, I could just tell that man had at least 8 inches to console me on my failing marriage. I knew this because of the many times I had stared at his crouch as he walked pass me, and the grey sweats he wore every Saturday to work out with a group at the church gym. His shoulders looked like I could sit all my troubles plus a few body parts of my choice on them.

On the other hand, as my doting husband never failed to remind me in his jealous fits, "God will punish the unfaithful". His suspicions only led me to believe that he himself had some outside dealings but since I had yet to discover the full truth of that revelation, I could only speculate.

*That being said, an eye for an eye, right? Or what he doesn't know, won't hurt me. Whichever would keep my conscious clear as I climbed this tree of a man and rode him like the very first cowgirl to do it. No, that wouldn't be right. I'm a married woman and a woman of God at that. No, I can get everything I need from my husband.* I reasoned with myself as the meeting came to an end.

I found myself waiting in the parking lot. Not for my husband, because he had other church business to attend to and had said he'd be home in a couple of hours. Not even for my children, they had left with my husband's relatives for the night. No, I was waiting for him. We had managed to make plans after my husband let me know not to expect him to leave with me. I spotted him making his way towards me and was immediately conflicted. I couldn't understand why because he wasn't the first man I had gone out with during my miserable ass marriage. I couldn't put my finger on it, but something was different about this time.

As this man walked towards me, my clit grew a pulse and I knew it was over for me.

"You ready to go?" His voice vibrated through me and tickled my pussy with anticipation.

I smiled. "Yes, I'm ready."

The end usually says a lot about the beginning. This was the beginning of the end. See what I didn't know was this time was different. After spending two hours having mind-blowing passionate sex...I stumble out to my car and drove home in a daze.

I managed to beat my husband home, but getting the scent and feel of that man off of me and out of my head proved to be a near impossible task. I was still in the shower when my husband walked in almost an hour after me.

When I came out, I found him at the dining room table going over his debut sermon. It had been all he was able to focus on for the past two weeks. So, I didn't have to worry about him noticing if I was acting any differently.

For the next three months, I crept into this man's bed and stumbled out more mesmerized than when I slipped in. He had all the heat I had dreamed of my husband having during those months before the wedding. He was becoming an addiction. When I wasn't with him, I wished I was; and when I was, I couldn't keep my hands...or mouth off of him. He was the same with me, He licked me so often that I could still feel his tongue strokes hours later. We had even begun to sneak away during church. My husband never noticed because his mind was always so heavily focused on church life and business. We were on sexual high until the inevitable happened.

We were spotted in his driveway saying our "goodbye" by one of the female church members. She had shown up to his house uninvited. She slithered out of her car. "Brother Aaron, Sister Pamela. What a nice surprise to catch...see you two together. Here at Brother Aaron's house." A fake smile plastered on her face.

"Hello, Sister Sheila. I don't remember giving you my address or saying that I was open to company." He smoothly shot back.

"Right, I got your address off of the church members lists. You know I'm on the board." She focused on him as she held a plate of what we could only guess was the cougar's plate of home-cooked flirtation.

"Sister Sheila, you still didn't say why you're here." He pressed.

"Excuse me, Sister Pamela." She brushed pass me. "I noticed you didn't make it to the weekly potluck; and I remember how much you liked my greens. So, I thought you'd appreciate me bringing you a plate."

I pretended to turn to walk away, making sure to knock her plate out of her hand and onto the ground between us. "Oh, I'm so sorry Sister Sheila."

"Sister Pamela, you never said what you're doing here at that this single brother's house. Did your husband send you here on church business?"

I could have slapped that old bitch. "Actually, my business here is done." I'll see you at church, Brother Aaron." I flashed a quick smile at him when she turned her attention his way.

"Yes, see you there… Sister." He said with a look that got my panties wet all over again…despite the soreness he had blessed me with.

As I rode home smiling, my mind wandered from the secret life I was living to all the dead things in my marriage. *So much of what we used to be had died over time, what did we have left?*

# **Chapter Nine**

## *The Last Death*

This entire time, my husband and I had continued to have problems. I kept asking if we were going to get more counseling and work at it, but he just kept saying he didn't know. He didn't know because he was seeing his high school sweetheart from back in Mississippi. She had moved out to LA and no one knew, except for my husband because they were a couple in another city. It was like a storyline off of a reality T.V show. Husband has a wife and kids in one city and a girlfriend in another. Well, at least he didn't have a child by her. Or did he? Either way, he was unaware that I had knowledge of his second family.

So, one night, he came home late. He was usually at the house by six or seven, but this night he came home about nine. Naturally, I asked him where he had been. He responded with, "We need to talk. I've talking with my best friend brother about what I should do about us since we were in Jacksonville. Ronnie says I should stay and work with you on us. I've been trying to go with his opinion, but it's gotten us nowhere. Jonathan has been telling me to get out of this sham of a marriage before things really go left. I've been watching things go exactly as he foretold." He paused then walked up to me and said that he wanted a divorce.

I was nonchalant about it, *I mean it was coming, right?* He went on to say that he knew I was cheating on him. Of course, my response was,

"Define cheating...because I'm sure you don't consider you and "T" cheating. Or, your high school sweetheart who lives in the same city you work in? Is whatever you and her have going on cheating? and if it's your brother we're listening to, at least know his motive."

His whole facial expression changed. "What you mean by that?"

"I mean, when we went back to Mississippi, he was trying to fuck me every time he saw me. He's sent me messages with a hotel name and room number. He's sent flowers and chocolate arrangements. He's popped up at many of my events that you didn't go to trying to feel me up... Ohhhh, and when he visited us a few days ago, he had every intention of licking all the rust out my pussy. So, yeah...your brother has motive. I decided to keep Aaron my little secret.

I saw the hurt in his eyes but instead of responding, he told me that his family prophet said that "The Lord showed her that I was going to blow me up in a car. That me and my boyfriend were going to put a bomb in his car and blow him up so that we could be together". *What a joke! First of all, my so-called "boyfriend" had a wife, so even with my husband dead and gone, we still couldn't have been together. So, I knew that was a lie. Secondly, we only had one car at this point.* His car had gotten repossessed because like I said, he was terrible with money and wasn't paying the bill that he said he was paying. (I don't know what the hell he was doing with the money). So, if you driving my car, ain't no way in hell I'm blowing up my only car because I want to kill you. Why the fuck would I blow somebody up anyway when I could just poison you? That was too stupid, it made no sense. I have a sociology degree; I've learned about cases of murder. So, I'm well aware of the things that I could use to put in his food. Not to mention the fact that he was already diabetic. I could kill him and it would be nothing, but when you're talking about

49

blowing someone up…don't you know that takes C4, dynamite and a whole lot of preparation. I ain't have preparation time, I didn't need preparation time to kill him. So, I'm more than positive that he had just come from his mother's house where he, his mother, the family prophet, who had listened to his brother's wife, had come up with a vision from the Lord saying all this stupid shit. That is what sparked his desire for a divorce.

That night I slept in the living room while he was in the bedroom. He came into the living room trying to have sex with me. In my mind, *muthafucka we ain't had sex in damn near six months. We only had sex three or four times a year. What the hell you coming in here for now? Are you serious? Get the hell on out of here.* What I said was, "You said our marriage had run it's course. Well, my pussy ran hers right along with that shit. So have a great life." Then I got to thinking, I had to let him know exactly what he would be missing. Plus, I was horny anyway. So, I let him lead me into the bedroom where I gave him the sloppiest head I had ever given him. I got on my knees in front of him and stared him right in the eyes as I swallowed him whole. All this time, I had been holding back not wanting him to feel self-conscious about his size. Now, as he stared at me like he had just tried crack for the first time, I realized I had it all wrong. I slurped and sucked until he was damn near comatose. Then, since he hadn't said a word, I gave new meaning to the phrase "cat got your tongue". I sat my pussy on his face, pinched his nipple until he opened his mouth and jerked and sucked his dick until he started licking. Six years, six long years and I hadn't gotten good head from him once. That night, it was a miracle on 21st street. I came all on his mouth and he drank it up like it was water from the fountain of youth. After I was satisfied with the job he had done with his tongue. I eased myself down on to his dick and we had some of the nastiest sex we had ever had. I started out bouncing on his lap. From there, he bent me over, and we finished with my legs on his shoulders. Every time it looked like he might cum, I would just pull him out of me, the disappointment and desire in his eyes was hilarious. I had to have cum at least six or seven times before finally I let his no-stamina having ass finish. *I should have taken control from the beginning.* When I walked out that bedroom, I had no doubt that he would be missing my ass. He would miss all of this goodness. Me and my kids left and we never went back to that apartment.

"Til death do us part." We all know the words, and every married couple has recited them. Very few know how true they are though. I wondered what deaths would part my husband and I? So much of who we were had died already. What would have to die before we went our separate ways?

# **Chapter Ten**

## *What Deaths Will Part You?*

*What deaths do we part?* So, in the six years we were together, what had run its course? Sex was a problem. Money was a problem, because of the spending…not that we lacked it. He was a country boy and I was country girl, he wanted me barefoot and pregnant which was a lot of the reason that I got my tubes tied right after having my son, but also in the birthing of my son…my cervix collapsed and I almost died. So, I didn't want to go through that. I tied them for heath reasons but I didn't want to have anymore kids for him because I didn't want to have ten kids running around in the world and we be looking stupid. *Who was going to raise them?*

*How many deaths will it take to give life to your marriage again or for it to end? How many are you going to allow before you say "fuck it. I'm done"? Spiritual death, financial death? Emotional? Mental? How many things have to die before you call it quits?* This is a question that can only be answered individually. What are you going to do to fix it? But how many people are still going to be willing to "fix it" when so many things are already dead? For us, a lot was dying within our marriage.

The problem that I had in this marriage was that I never forgot my needs, I wanted to be loved, I wanted to be held and kissed on. I wanted to have good hot, nasty sex and my husband couldn't give me that. I wanted us to be financially stable and we were but his spending was out of control. We had no understanding of each other or between us. We weren't communicating or understanding what was being said. We didn't comprehend each other. Whether we were talking calmly or out of anger. We took so many measures to try to "fix" our marriage, we went to four counseling sessions both before and during our marriage to revive it. So, we had the mind to fix it but either our egos or age or the fact that we were just on different levels contributed to every that was meant to be in a marriage parting. So, we had so many deaths that parted us, that it was so far gone that it was unrepairable.

It sounds like that's the end of my story, but really that's just the beginning. My life started when my marriage died. I used what I went through and learned to help other couples all over the country through my syndicated television show, "Morning Cup with PJ and Crew".

On this episode, I am sitting with four couples. We're playing the newly-wed game. I ask the couples four questions to get them laughing and having fun.

"Question number one is for Miranda and Jonathan. If you were an M&M, what color would you be?"

Jonathan held a board to his chest, while Miranda answered. "PJ, my man would be the red M&M." Jonathan turns over his board and they high five each other.

"The next question is for Jason and Latesha. How friendly is your alter ego?"

Latesha smiled wide as Jason held the board to his chest. "Super friendly, might as well be an angel." Jason turns over his board and the audience burst into laughter.

"Oh no! Sorry Latesha, your answer doesn't match Jason's." I held in a chuckle.

"She's a bitch!?" Latesha read the board out loud. "Jason, I can't believe you!"

"Our third question is for Nicolette and Antonio. If you were a roach, which kind of roach would you be?"

Nicolette frowned before she answered. "I wouldn't be a roach at all. I'm more like a butterfly, graceful and beautiful." Antonio sucked his teeth as he flipped his board and said, "She be a Mexican hissing roach because she's always ready to attack." Nicolette snatched the board and beat Antonio over the head with it. "Fuck you!" They fight their way off the stage as the audience reacts.

"Wow, okay. Back to the game. We still have three couple that can win the Jamaica baecation getaway. Let's move into the next segment. This question is for you, Katrina and Ray. If your partner died and you were looking down at them for the last time. What would you say to them?"

A smirk took over Ray's face. "I'd finally tell her that I've been sleeping with her sister Dena for the past six months and her baby is mine."

The audience burst out in noise as Dena jumped out of her seat and kicked Ray in his chest causing him and his chair to fall backwards. Security stormed the stage, but I just smiled and kept the show going.

"You never know what will happen here on The Morning Cup with PJ and the Crew! Dena may not have known it but I always ask the right questions. Now she knows!" I laugh and watch my security team escort Dena and Ray off the stage. "Even though my question seems harsh, it could happen when you walk out these doors. You have to love those that love you. Life is too short and we are going to have days we are tired. We are going to have days we are sad or mad or disappointed. But we have to choose to let love and happiness win. Keep it in the back of your heads that death is just a blink away. And when death comes, it's truly a lifetime gone." I stood up and prepared to change the mood of the audience and couples. "Looks like we are headed right into our "royal rings" round. The couple that wins this round will be headed to Jamaica for an all-inclusive seven-day-six-night baecation. Y'all ready to win?" I turned to the last two couples.

"Yes!" Three of the four on stage said in unison; but the fourth, Miranda said, "No."

I returned to my seat beside the couples. "Why not, Miranda. Do you have something you want to get off your chest too?" I asked, already knowing the answer because she had mentioned it to me before we went on the air.

"Yes, I do." She turned toward her husband with tears in her eyes. "You know we've been having some issues conceiving since before the wedding and it's been a touchy subject for me. I know it's caused so much friction between us and I want to thank you for how patient you've been the entire time." The audience all said "awe" on cue. She continued. "I also want to tell you on national television that in about 34 weeks, you're going to be a daddy."

Jonathan jumped up out of his seat and scooped her up in his arms. "Are you fucking kidding me?!" He screamed out in excitement and tongue kissed her.

"Jonathan…I can imagine the feelings welling up inside you but we have to keep in mind we are on the air. Let's keep it PG13."

"Right, I'm sorry PJ." Jonathan said as they sat back down.

I walked across the stage and asked the last question of the show. "What is the most important element in your marriage?"

After congratulating Miranda and Jonathan on their bundle of joy in the oven and sent Jason and Latesha on their way to Jamaica, we dismissed with a promise. "I promise to be the best partner I can be. I will be better from this day forward. I will love my partner daily as if today is our last day. I'll love myself so that I can be the best partner I can be and I will remain open to change and growth within my relationship." The couple, the audience and I all said in unison.

As I walked outside, someone called my name and I was frozen in my tracks. The smooth and sexy voice was all too familiar. I turned around to find a delivery truck parked in the middle of the studio parking lot. My heart skipped a beat…

"Mack?"

Made in the USA
Middletown, DE
13 September 2022

72964435R00038